Sonia Levitin
A Piece of Home

Pictures by Juan Wijngaard

Dial Books for Young Readers New York

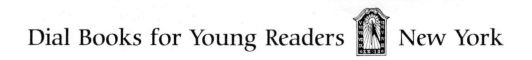

*In loving memory of my mother, who brought
me to America, and for my sister Eva with love*

S.L.

To Ruslan, Nuryyev, Felix, and Lurye

J.W.

꿃껟꿃껟

Published by Dial Books for Young Readers
A Division of Penguin Books USA Inc.
375 Hudson Street
New York, New York 10014

Design by Nancy R. Leo
Printed in the U.S.A.
First Edition
1 3 5 7 9 10 8 6 4 2

Library of Congress Cataloging in Publication Data
Levitin, Sonia, 1934–
A piece of home / by Sonia Levitin; pictures by Juan Wijngaard.
p.   cm.
Summary: Gregor decides to take his special blanket when his family leaves
Russia to live in America, but he worries about his choice all during the journey.
ISBN 0-8037-1625-7.—ISBN 0-8037-1626-5 (lib. bdg.)
[1. Emigration and immigration—Fiction. 2. Russian Americans—Fiction.]
I. Wijngaard, Juan, ill. II. Title.
PZ7.L58Pi 1996   [E]—dc20   93-42243   CIP   AC

*The art for this book was prepared with watercolors. It was then
color-separated and reproduced in red, yellow, blue, and black halftones.*

A *garmoshka* is a musical instrument, a small accordian with
round buttons instead of pianolike keys. A *samovar* is an urn with
a little faucet at its bottom, used to heat water for tea.

Gregor and his family are moving to America. They have waited for a long, long time.

"When we go to America," says Gregor's mother, "you will see your cousin Elie. He is the same age as you."

Ever since Gregor was a baby, he has heard about Cousin Elie. On Mama's bureau is a picture of Cousin Elie with Aunt Marissa and Uncle Ivan. They are standing in front of a small wooden house in America. Around the house are some trees and a fence.

Gregor has never seen a house like this. He lives in an apartment building with many floors and an elevator and the sounds of other families singing through the halls. Cousin Elie's house in America looks strange. Gregor is not sure he wants to go there.

✧✧✧

But the time has come. They must pack. Gregor has a suitcase of his own.

"We cannot take much," says Mama.

"Only one special treasure for each of us," says Papa. "Something to share with our family in America."

Baby Katje takes her teething ring made of elk horn. This she will not share.

Papa says, "I must take my garmoshka, for how could I live in America without music?"

Mama says, "I will take our small samovar. My sister Marissa always loved our good Russian tea." Whenever Mama talks about her sister Marissa, she looks as if she will start to cry.

Gregor does not know what to take to America. The beautiful painted chair his father's friend made for him? The ice skates that are still almost new? The brass harness bells he loves to hear on a winter's night?

Gregor does not want to leave anything behind. But Mama and Papa say he must choose. It is too expensive to bring everything to America. Besides, in a new land people like new things.

The last night arrives. Still Gregor cannot decide what to take. Papa is cross. Mama wrings her hands. Even Baby Katje is fussy.

When Gregor is cold or tired or unhappy, he knows what to do. He runs and gets the blanket Great-grandmother made. It is warm and soft and pretty.

Gregor gathers up the blanket. "I will take this to America," he says.

Mama looks tired. "It is too big to pack," she says.

"I will carry it," says Gregor.

"It will get dirty," Mama says.

Papa says, "Look, if you come with a blanket, your cousin Elie will think you are a baby."

Gregor says, "I want my blanket."

Mama sighs and looks at Papa.

Papa nods and says, "Very well. At least it is settled."

The long journey begins at the airport, filled with noise. The plane starts with a loud roar. Baby Katje screams, and Mama tries to rock her to sleep.

Gregor sits between Mama and Papa, holding tight to the seat belt around his middle. The sky turns dark. Gregor is almost asleep, but they have to leave this plane and wait for another plane to take them to America.

Gregor is so tired. He wishes he were home. He lies down on a chair, wrapped in his blanket.

At last they get onto another plane. It is cold. Gregor puts his blanket over his head and sleeps.

The smell of food wakes him. Supper comes on little white plastic trays. Gregor likes the potatoes and the round white roll and the golden peaches. The other food tastes strange.

"Eat your meat," says Mama. "Eat your beans."

Gregor shakes his head. "I'm not hungry," he says. "I want to go home." He feels tears in his eyes.

A nice lady brings him small toys. There is a tiny airplane, crayons, a coloring book. But Gregor does not feel like playing. He is thinking of his friends at home, and of his teacher at day school. Now Gregor is sure he does not want to go to America. But he tells the lady "thank you," new words he has learned. His cousin Elie speaks perfect English. He also speaks Russian. Everyone says how smart Elie is in school.

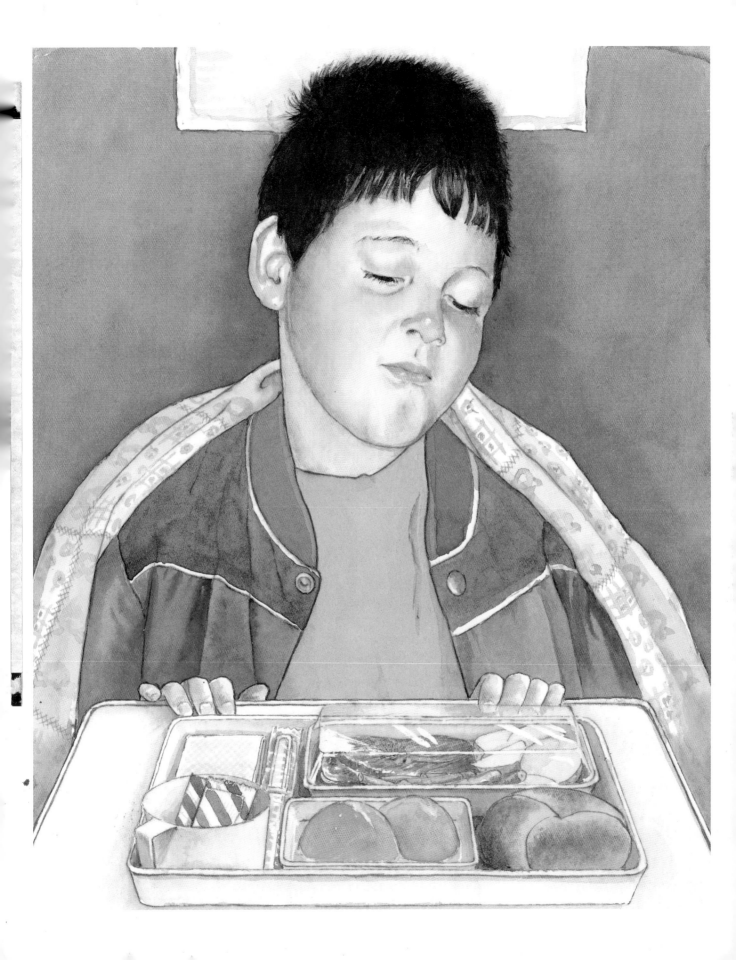

Why do they have to go to America? Gregor has asked his parents many times.

"In America," Papa says proudly, "work is waiting for me." Papa works with wood, making beautiful cabinets.

"In America," Mama says happily, "we will not be lonely. We will be with our family."

Now Gregor pulls his blanket tight around himself. Finally he sleeps again.

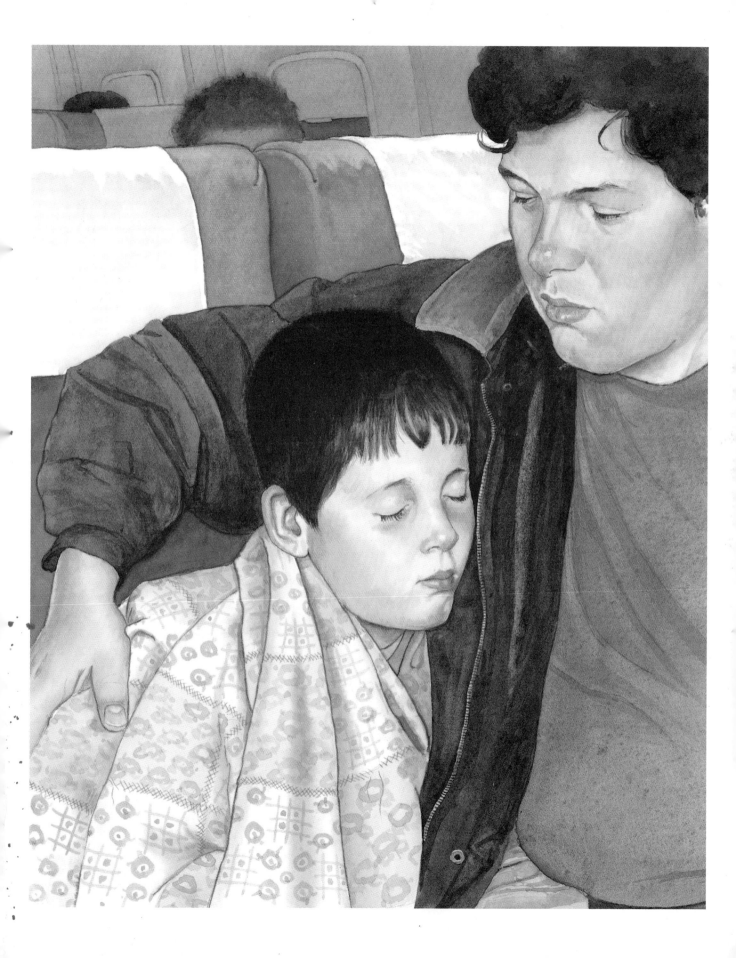

"Wake up!" Papa says. "We're almost there."

Light comes into the plane. People stretch and find their things.

Baby Katje is fast asleep.

Gregor feels a flutter in his stomach. Will he like Cousin Elie? Gregor looks down at the blanket. There is a hole in it. The colors are faded. Gregor wishes he had listened to Papa and left the blanket at home. But it is too late.

Mama folds the blanket into a small bundle and puts it in Gregor's lap.

Now Gregor is sure that Cousin Elie will laugh at him and call him a baby. Maybe he should just leave the blanket here on the airplane. Gregor cannot decide.

With a rush of sound, a swoop of motion, the plane lands. Papa leads the family out of the plane.

"Are we here?" asks Gregor. "Where is Cousin Elie?"

But nobody answers him. Papa and Mama are busy with passports and papers. They wait in line so long that Gregor's foot goes to sleep. At last they move out to a large room. A man and a woman rush over. The man catches Gregor and holds him up high. The woman covers Gregor's face with kisses. The woman smiles, then weeps, then laughs. She looks a little like Mama.

"Welcome! Welcome to America!" say Aunt Marissa and Uncle Ivan.

Katje squeals and claps her hands. Everyone laughs.

Now Gregor sees the little boy standing behind Aunt Marissa.

"What's the matter with you, Elie?" says Aunt Marissa. "Come out and say hello!"

Mama gives Gregor a little push and tells him, "Gregor, this is your cousin Elie. Say hello!"

Cousin Elie says hello in the small voice of a mouse. He is wearing boots and a leather vest with fringes, just like a cowboy. Gregor tries to hide his blanket behind his back; it is too big.

The men talk and laugh. The women hug and kiss, then Aunt Marissa takes Baby Katje in her arms. Gregor does not like the way Cousin Elie is looking at him.

"Why are we standing here?" shouts Uncle Ivan. "Come on! Let's go!"

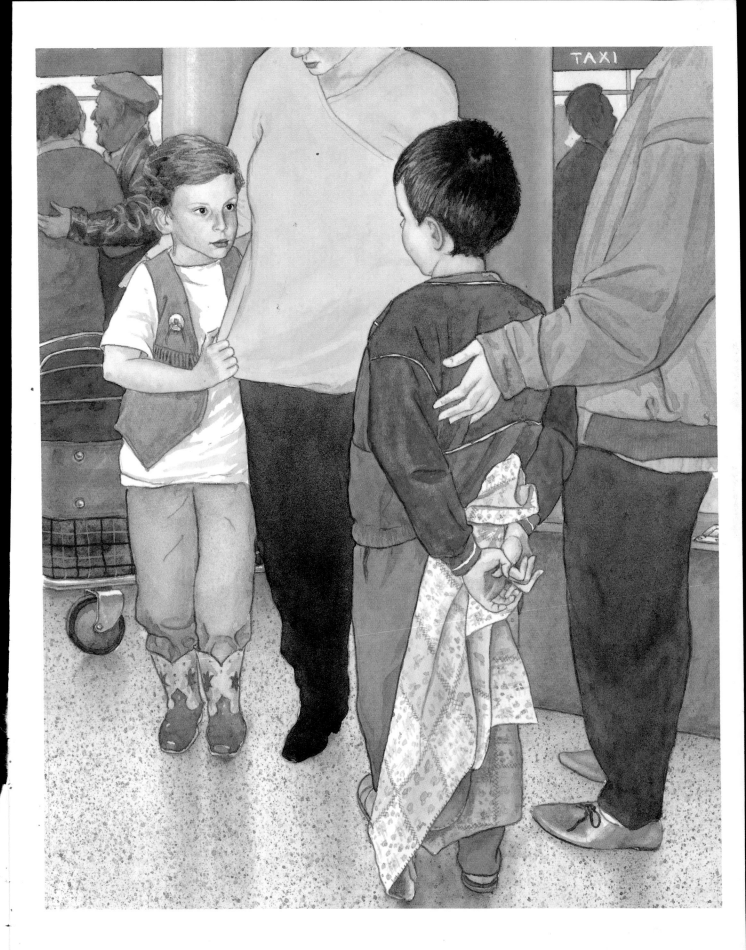

Everyone squeezes into Uncle Ivan's car, with suitcases on top and in between. Gregor sits on Papa's lap, still holding his blanket. Cousin Elie sits in front with his parents.

Soon they stop at a house. It is so big! "Five rooms," says Uncle Ivan, laughing and nodding. "Five rooms! Well, well, that's how it is in America. Soon you will have a house of your own. In the meantime you will stay with us."

First they eat. There is plenty. Gregor feels empty inside, but he eats only one olive and a cracker.

Cousin Elie eats and stares at Gregor.

Uncle Ivan brings in the coffee.

Aunt Marissa says, "Ah, I remember the good Russian tea we used to make from the samovar at home."

Mama jumps up. When she comes back, she is holding the small samovar, smiling like a queen.

Aunt Marissa fills it with water for tea.

Uncle Ivan pats his full belly and says, "There is nothing like a song after a meal."

Papa hurries out. In a moment he is back holding his garmoshka, already playing and singing.

The grown-ups all sing.

At home Gregor would sing too. But Cousin Elie is staring at him, making faces. Now Gregor wishes he had never come to America. Gregor pulls his blanket close to his chest. He wants to hide inside it and never come out.

The song ends. Suddenly Cousin Elie points at Gregor and shouts, "That's my blanket!"

"No," cry all the parents. "Of course not. How could it be?"

Aunt Marissa comes close to Gregor. She bends down to look at the blanket. Softly she asks Mama, "Is this the blanket Great-grandmother made?"

"Yes," says Mama. "Great-grandmother gave it to our mother on her wedding day."

Aunt Marissa is laughing now. "I remember when I was a little girl. Mama wrapped me up in that blanket."

Papa says, "When Gregor was born, we carried him home in that blanket."

"At one time," Mama says, "the blanket was twice as big. I don't know what happened to the rest."

Aunt Marissa and Cousin Elie whisper together. "Wait!" says Aunt Marissa. She and Cousin Elie run upstairs.

When they return, Cousin Elie has a funny look on his face. He is wearing a blanket exactly like Gregor's.

Aunt Marissa says, "We cut the blanket in half, so I could bring a piece of home with me to America. Don't you remember?"

Now Mama is drying her eyes. "I don't remember a thing," she says, "except how much I missed you."

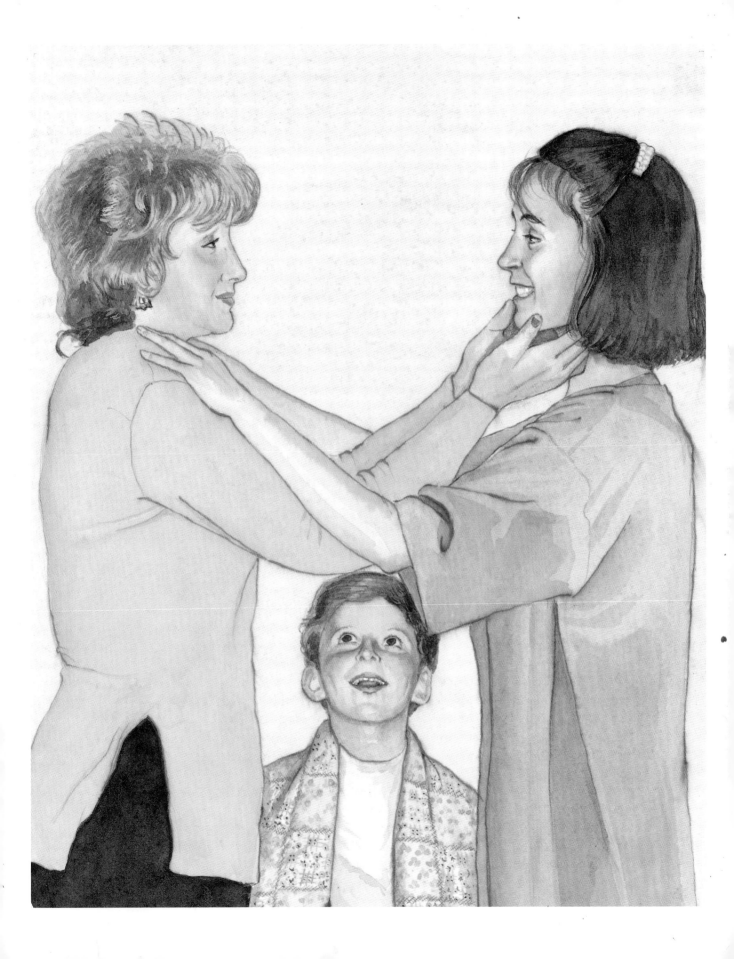

Elie takes Gregor by the arm. "Want to go out and play?" he asks.

"Okay," says Gregor. It was the first English word he ever learned. "Okay!" says Gregor once again. He likes the sound of this word. It is very American. It makes him smile.